The Garden Black

and other speculations

Frank Prem

Wild Arancini Press
2022

Publication Details

Title: The Garden Black

ISBN: ISBN: 978-1-925963-50-2 (p-bk)
ISBN: 978-1-925963-80-9 (e-bk)

Published by Wild Arancini Press
Copyright © 2022 Frank Prem
All rights reserved:

A catalogue record for this book is available from the National Library of Australia.

Cover Concept: Wild Arancini Press
Cover Image AI assistant: Adobe Firefly

from a single root
all the roads of the universe
run

CONTENTS

The Garden Black

The Garden Black

Introduction

The Garden Black poetry collection is a venture into fantasy and speculative fiction that arose from the desire to write a worthy submission for inclusion in an anthology of stories based on the dual themes of rain forest and fantasy.

One idea turned into a multitude of stories:

The rainforest becomes a desert, and then the sea.

A man in a satellite orbits the earth while playing his violin and pondering. A girl gazes up at the passing light and dances.

Od Ovo - a youth who is *from here,* raises the dust of frustrated boredom on a mining asteroid, and cannot believe traveller tales of places where water falls from the sky.

What colour are the flowers in the Reaper's garden? They are *all* colours . . .

They are black.

Welcome to the speculative fantasies that are *The Garden Black.*

being foolish

this
is not a job
you know

this is being
what
I am

I collect the beads
the shiny baubles

I lay the pattern
so . . .

just so

and this bead
must be placed
there

any other way
is foolish

I
am not
foolish

and when
my bower is completely . . .

so . . .

with the design
of me
laid down
at the door

I will
preen
for you

I
will show

     my chest

     my tail

     my neck my eyes

     my colour

I dance now
I dance . . .

look at me
the way
I dance

and I dance

this
is not
a foolish thing

I am
who I am

cello

   mmmm
   hmmmm
   mmmm

mellow notes
to touch me

   hmmmm

notes
to call me
to life

   mmmm
   hmmmm

these notes
sound low
and I sing

a heart song

of release

   hmmmm
   mmmm

cello . . .

I . . .

one song

one player

   mmmm mmmm . . .

Frank Prem

a song for the (low) horizon

I play
to the crowd
below
as I pass

quicker
than a breathless sigh

they slip away
until they are
horizon

until
they disappear
down
and beyond
the far side
of the planet

no one notices

no one
cares

I am anonymous

a man alive
unchanging
in his own cocoon

if they look
they'll see a shooting star
hurtling
through the night

a reflection
a kind of deflection
of the sun

I take my fiddle
out of the case
that I keep taped
to the wall

catch the escaping rosin

apply it
to the bow

limber my voice
up
and down
and
deeper

then an exercise
for fingers

my left hand
fingers

danny boy

I always begin
with a rendition
of *danny boy*
followed by a brief dance tune
then . . .

in just a short while
I start singing

everything that is *me*
that is my *voice*
fills the capsule
with my singing

sound
gets lost in space
or so they say

but
if I position myself
in the right place
in the *best* place
my voice . . .

echoes

it comes back
at me

and I sound
as though
I am a harmony

come
jig a little jig
for me
while I play

I think I can imagine
just the way
you'd dance

I will sing for you
a space-station solo

all by myself

in a kind of harmony

.

.

.

I look down
through the port
again

you
and your world
are gone

there is a silver line
along the low horizon

leaf and leave

I watch the leaves
through the air

they are
falling

autumn
is gone

winter
yet grips
the spring

here
the sun shines down
empty of the warm I knew
before this season

another one
falls

I can't help
my awe

grace
in death
rolls
freely
on the breeze

and I wonder . . .

does no leaf
now
wish to stay
snugged
close to the bough

our sky

I and the cloud
stand
shoulder
next to shoulder

I am the eagle
the cloud
is the wind
to fly

if I leap
my arms spread
wide as I can
the cloud will glide
underneath my body

hold me up
in the air

two of us
as one

ours alone
is the widening sky

ours alone
is the wide

wide

wide

blue sky

the children

oh
such a child
of fury

oh child
child
of anger

a turbulence
of joy denied

a storm
of boiling rage

oh such a child
so much
displeasure

> *look at them*
> *fall*
> *it was I*
> *who felled them*
>
> *look at them dry*
> *it was my will*
> *that withheld*
>
> *look . . .*
>
> *watch the dust-witch*
> *rising*
>
> *so much*
> *do I despise*

the sky above me
is a burn
in the blue

there will be
no weeping

~

child
can you smell
the water

child child
can you not smell
each droplet
of the rain

you weep
when you feel joy

and you weep
when you
are thwarted
but . . .

there is love
within
when you are walking

look at the green . . .

something
grows there

look at the way
it rises
to my touch

look
do you see
how lovely
after rain

the more I see
the more
I wish

above me
the sky is deep
and blue
and filled
with the drift
of billowing clouds

my tears
are shaded
in colours

every colour
that is
the rainbow

searching myself (river to sea)

you
are a river
running

I
am the blue sky
above

I watch
your silver ribbons
dance

and I see you
laughing

reflections
of sunlight

~

I am the blue
I reach up
to touch starlight

higher
again
to find the feeling
of night

I reach deep

into myself
to the pound
of my own heart
beating

and I find you
I reach you
there
in a place I keep
inside me

~

I
am the blue
you
are the heartbeat

flow
my river
I will watch you
to the sea

I who am

leaf and bough
the forest floor
lies somewhere
down below

I can feel it
when I turn
inward
to my senses

but up here
should a breeze
move my leaves

I am overtaken
by the feeling
of a sway

of dancing
by myself
with just the sun

root and bark
the canopy moves
while I hold on
to the ground

I am the source
that lives
in darkness

I send up water

I send up food
I cling
to sustain

in my perpetuality
of night
I feel the pleasure
that sways above
and I
am at peace

sap and wood
this is
what it means
to be a forest

push
and stretch

I grow higher

I know the wind
I know the sun
I know the dark
beneath the soil

leaf and bough

root and bark

sap and wood

I am tree

I
am forest

coming up

climb
a ladder of raindrops

to take you
up
to the cloud

then through
until
the sky

dance your dance
of stamping feet

just
as the raindrops stamp
when they reach
the ground

or
splash down
on my hand

the sun is shining
I don't see it
from here but
you . . .

up
on the cloud tops
you
can lift your head

close your eyes

touched by rays
of gold
and warm

hold that ladder

steady . . .

steady there now

I
am coming

so
hold the rain
quiet too

hold it still

I am coming

the hunter writes a letter

he writes
as a hunter writes

a letter
to the spoor
of his prey

> *I see where*
> *you*
> *have been*
>
> *what*
> *you have done*
>
> *I see where*
> *I*
> *will catch you . . .*

she reads
like
a sprite of the forest
her tinkling laughter
fills the air

just as a stream
she runs

> *I am*
> *everywhere*
>
> *you*
> *will never find me*

I
am every
where . . .

he studies
the disturbances

leaf litter

scratchings
across the path

with every sign
he draws a little
nearer . . .

.

.

.

she watches
from the epiphytes

splashes in bromeliads

dances on the barely
paths

keeps the game alive . . .

he holds an image
of her
in the trophy cabinet
of his mind . . .

and so the hunt
the dream
progresses

written
to the prey

laughed
like the sun
leaping off water

swell

in the echo
that is *mellish street*
the sound
is someone swimming

freestyle

a snort exhaled
a gulp inhumed
deeply

then backstroke
just above the road
legs
kicking fury

the ordinary sounds
of evening
in *mellish street*

this swimmer
must be
a kind of convoy
for the noise of him
seems unceasing

butterfly stroke
the asphalt
yields its ground
to the wave of force
and to the swimmer

listen now
there is a boat
that is a car
waking to the shore
as it drives the tidal road
swim
little fish

swim you must

this swell
for you
is a kind of drowning

one
by one
the cars set
to cruise control

the swimmer
keeps on driving

this swell

is risen up
for a drowning

bitter

the cold falls down
in sheets
and flakes
of shivers

mounded
outside the door

it rattles
like a demand for entrance
that would strip me

naked
I approach the flame

naked I seek
the warm

and naked
here am I . . .

white powder
on my shoulders
an epaulette insignia
of bitterness

the clack and the ah

my breath makes a

>   *clack*

when it goes in

every exhale
is a sigh

lying
with my eyes closed
I am a world
of

>   *clack*

and

>   *ahhh*

>   *(ah-ah-ah-ahhh)*

I do not really
breathe

I am ven air
I am . . .

inspired

to focus

I can feel my chest
inflate
to focus

I know the rise
of ribs
I know the fall

infinity rolls
into the space
that is a pause
between

    ah-ahhh

    (ah-ah-ah-ahhh)

and the

    clack

that is my new air

every sound
is heightened

into the only sense
still
to remain

but
I don't hear

nothing at all

only

    clack

only

ahhh

(ah-ah-ah-ahhh)

clack

ahhh

(ah-ah-ah-ahhh)

storm and the sea (bubbles of foam)

I called to joe
I said

> *there's a boat*
> *trying to fly*
> *right out of the water*

the wind
had taken a breath
and it was
blowing

even as I spoke
I saw a wave
lift up that vessel

then
crash it down
like a fragile toy
built poor
by some clumsy child

~

there is no light
to speak of
when you're staring
at the heart
of the storm

grey-black cloud
and green water

the white —
maybe —
of salt

even a man
is just a pale thing

a dark shape

a nothing at all
but the brilliant
shrieking song

of a wild wind

~

joe took me
by the arm

said

    nothing here

    nothing left

    there is only
    the sea

not even a board
from the decking
made it to shore

not a cry
that didn't hail
from the wind of hell itself

nothing left
but storm
and the sea

some bubbles
of foam

I dig (a forest)

I am digging
a hole
through dirt
and broken bricks

there was a tree
here
once before

I
am excavating
the place
to plant another

~

I eat . . .
a tree goes down

I shit . . .
there goes one more

I can't blow my nose
for fear
I might cost the world
a forest

put on my working pants . . .
zip
I fell a conifer

wear a shirt in checks . . .
that one
was a hardwood

I shouldn't breathe
anymore
it has become
so damned expensive

~

pick me up
take me
by the hand

carry me
at tree-top height

I will run
my fingers
through the leaves
to touch
some kind of reassurance

~

I don't want to be the one
to down
the last of the trees

so
I dig another dark hole
into the ground

through the broken bricks
and dirt

through fractured bottles

~

once there was
a tree

once
there was
a forest

in the sand (lost at sea)

here
in the dunes
I fear
I may be drowning

in shimmers
of sun . . .

of light

my heart beats
the sand

and I will write you
a letter
penned
through dust
that fills my hands
to say

> *your name*
> *is the one*
> *I am calling*

~

and
I have swum
pushing the grains
away from me

to make
such progress
my whole body
was immersed

the wide wake
streamed out
behind me
shows the great circle
I have travelled

and
have crossed again
and again
on my path

the sand
is no liar

~

> *what of the sharks*
>
> *what*
> *of the serpents*

the wavering sun
reveals them
clear

they are creatures
insubstantial
sounding
from the deeps
of my brain

for each word
I pen
another will consume me

~

I wonder
at last

>   *what is left*
>   *of the man*
>   *I was*

here
there is only a soul
lost
far out at sea

still I swim
through swelling dunes

what else
to do . . .

I am marooned

~

I place this letter
of my love
now
into the care
of the desert ocean

pride (in a sister)

we hunt
we are pride
my sister and me

I cough
politely
to gain attention

I speak my name
a little louder
into the wind

politely

to gain
attention

I am the *minister*
to this
my little flock

I pray —
aloud —
to draw their attention

politely
politely

I have certain things
to say

I speak
into
their attention

oh
let us pray

oh oh
oh let us pray . . .

ah
my dear
you have our prey

and I need
no more
their attention

sister mine
it is pride
we are

politely
let us prey

will believe

will the sun
to shine in the dark

will the moon
to rise
at first light

will *every hour*
of waking
to
another time . . .

a *different*
time

let me sleep now

I have things
to do

and wake me up
for I wish
to start my dreaming

night time
into day

sleep time
I am *awake*

right time
is wrong
so *wrong*

I *will* my heart
into believing

it is not clear (from the dream below)

it is not
clear
when I look
to the heavens

I do not see
sky
in the places
in the ways
that I should

I see
wavering

I see swirls
and light

hovering
somewhere above
the air line

~

I make the bubble
that is my breath

rise

to escape me

a fin
right now
would serve me well

in its absence
I push myself forward
by a surge
of will

~

what
is the time

what is
my time

it is difficult
to judge
gauging only
by shipwreck

and what
is the hour . . .

when I see
that the *big fish*
are feeding
I know

and what am *I*
down here
at last
when I *dream*
that I should be
walking

~

above the soapy tide
up on the sand
where breezes
blow

I dream that
once
I was a man
and owned it all

once

in a *when*
that meant something . . .

precious

but now
I hold on

cling fast
to the disappearance . . .

to the fading
of a dream

fearful
I may wake
to a vision

dressed
exactly the way
I am

a song for the (far) horizon

she would watch the sky
at night
at those times
when the moon seemed small

sometimes
the outline was there
in full
even though a crescent
was all that shone
in reflected-sun light

then
she would spend long minutes
reassuring herself
which specks were planets
which
were stars

couldn't reconcile
why only some pinpoints
would twinkle

venus
always seemed a little like
a lover circling
round the moon

sometimes near
sometimes
at a distance

and then
some other times
a star would move
right to left
across her sky

she wondered
when she saw it

    was it a ship

    a station

or just a satellite
picturing the glow
of cities

and she wondered
if a man up there
could look down
and see her home
all the way down here
on earth

marvelled
at the haste of light
shooting through the darkness

in its scurry
to the far side
of the world

then
she danced
a little sub-lunar dance

legs
and arms
and dizzying twirls

looked up again
to see venus
and the moon

only a few stars
twinkling

found by the ocean

the ocean of the road
is quiet now

no car splash
for quite a while

I love
to play in the waves
that sound makes

dive below a breaker

or
let the foam
wash over my feet

the tides
can be treacherous
when there is traffic

sun is on the bitumen now
though its rays
still carry
a seasonal chill

another car
makes a driving
splash

the sound expands
to find me

the ocean
swells up again

to find me

a vision above grey

there is a smoke
upon the hills

it wreathes them
till they
are only cloud

a parting by the breeze
shows a rising slope
that is the path
to *mountain*

another bite of wind
closes gaps
into a solid grey
that speaks words
translated

into *forbidding*

so that I must wonder
did I really see
the way

did I see
a summit
rising

~

I live life
in a kind of braille
I see
but cannot read
signs

forgive me
if I touch you

I am only
attempting a decryption

~

there is a vision
I can recall to my
front-of-mind

it is of myself
as a young man

climbing

the clouds
again
were low
but
my feet were sure
and steady

then
suddenly
the sunlight

a carpet layer
of brilliant white

thick fog
is all it was

I sat
on a stone
above it
engaged in the beauty

it is only
a recollected vision
and something
a little like
a dream

but
I will hold
to my hopes
that the grey
might give way to light . . .

to white

yes
I will take such hopes
wherever I
may find them

something

excuse me
I have lost something

I can't tell
where
I put it

something . . .
I have left something
behind

who are you
have you seen my . . .

I don't know

but should you see it
it is mine

was it only
yesterday
I had everything

at my fingertips

was it only . . .

no
when that was
I can't recall
but
something is gone
and I don't know . . .

I can feel it
will you help me
search

somewhere . . .

somewhere
quite near

hello
who are you

have you seen . . .

something . . .

I don't know . . .

a line of destiny

he wrote his fate
each day
in a book
onto a page
of sand

he didn't know . . .

how *could* he
know
what was yet
to come

but he made his lines
with a finger
held straight
as a pen
and with that
he made his marks

sometimes
the lines formed
into a picture

sometimes
he almost felt
a story being told
around him

sometimes the lines
looked a lot
like *himself*
when he gazed
into a mirror

and sometimes he
knew
that a line
is just a line

he drew a short-lived
line of destiny
every day
in a book
on a page of sand

only the wind
knew
how to read it

and when it was read
blew it all
away

pain control

my life i
s pain control

I don't live it
all that well

sometimes . . .

most times
the day comes to me
too fiercely

too loud

and I can stay in bed
close my eyes
not sleeping

or I could rise
to feel the hard beat
and the heavy
of my heart

~

> tablet in
> (and tablet in)
>
> tablet me again
> please
>
> only . . .
>
> only make this one
> much stronger

~

winter is a cold
white burn

it sears
what I once understood
was soul

I try
not to believe me
anymore

~

> *tablet in*
> *(and tablet in)*

~

footsteps
outside my bedroom door
somebody
has come
to wake me

shake me

break me

~

> *tablet in*
> *(and tablet in)*

> *and tablet me*
> *again*
> *and again and again*

~

leave me alone

the fog

I wondered —
as I watched —
where the day
had gone

the grey
above
had become
the grey
right here

and
as it drifted down
to hold me
too close
I felt the kiss of it

chilled
by a love
dressed
in mist droplets
swirling . . .

agitated

I *felt* the agitation

grasping
groping
trying
to touch me
at once
and all over

what could I do
but stand
with my eyes closed

mouth closed

heart closed

mind sent
to some other
world

until
it left me

bereft
and so alone

some
where
I know

the sun
shines

some where I know
the sun
shines

somewhere I know
and I *know*
the sun must be shining
so brightly

61

how long
will this fog
keep holding me

forever

garden black

I stroll
through the garden
black

the rose
is the smell
of night

touch a petal
feel it
before it falls

~

I wear a cape
the hood drawn
always
forward
to conceal my face

to sharpen my
implement
I
hone the dew

I
hone
the due

~

what is the time

has your time
flown
time
is a still thing
here

in the garden
I smell a rose

touch one petal
before
it falls

first a riffle

I saw the sun
spike up

it threw
a questing flame
far away
from the core

and I saw
then
a ripple
that was solar wind
speeding
from that distant star
toward me

now
I wait
my arms held wide
for the kiss of the sun
to find me

I wait
arms out
to burn

they say
a nautical man
could rig
a ship
and a special sail
to ride before the breeze
that I see coming

all the way
from hell
but I
am a pedestrian

and I stand ready
on this judging day
to meet my fate

first
a riffle of the air

and then
I burn

I (take the sun)

I rise
above the earth

mouth gaping

> *where*
> *is water*

stretch my wings
so
I can fly

mother mother
I leave you behind
dirt
falling from my roots

now is the time
to rise

I am leaving

touch the sky
kiss the stars
swallow whole
a yellow sun

move my wings
I am
a bird
of the empty spaces

see me swim
watch me
fly

I

I

I
will be
the fire

jet on night

he
is a silhouette

> *she*
> *a shadow leaning*
> *up against*
> *the wall*

he reaches
to touch her
with the sun
shining
behind him

> *she holds up*
> *a phantom hand*
> *to better feel*
> *their connection*

> *darkness on darkness*

he isn't there

> *jet on jet*

> *she isn't there*

the sun sets
they are gone again

melted away
by the breath

the first breath
of night

stirring before the rain

he blows
a puff of smoke
that hovers
just above his head

as though he is
about to start raining

a private
tropical storm

low hanging cloud

maybe a fog

his contemplation
is shallow
focused as it is
on the ascension
of a twisting plume
of blue . . .

of grey

he notices
the glow fade
from the heart
of his hand-held
small volcano

changing from

fired-up . . .

to

dormant . . .

ashen

nothing says

alive

like the smoke rising
from between the yellow
of knuckles gone hard
into brown

the colour
creates an impression
of long
hard labour

of regular performance
in *the-great-
outdoors*

but he pushes that aside
with a slight
sideways motion
of tongue inside mouth

coughs up
a modest accumulation

expectorates it
onto the ground beside him
and stirs himself

needing to move
before the rain

so he leaves

the hovering smoke
remains
but . . .
cigarette
and man
are only an aura silhouette
of vacant space
underneath a cloud

isosceles and me (and the war over the pond)

<background unobtrusive: soft tattoo on a single snare>

> *. . . ta*
> *ta-ta-ta-ta*
> *ta-ta-ta-ta*
> *ta-ta-ta*
> *ta*
> *ta*
>
> *ta*
> *ta-ta-ta-ta*
> *ta-ta-ta-ta*
> *ta-ta-ta*
> *ta*
> *ta . . .*

~

. . . well
it was a war

we all knew
we were fighting
for real

matt-o
and *davey* . . .

yeah
they didn't come back

'*fly-boys*

we were brothers

we were
the best
of the *'fly-boys*

we flew and we fought

won mostly

sometimes
we lost

but
it was a *war*
we were waging

~

     . . . *ta*

     ta-ta-ta-ta

     ta-ta-ta-ta

     ta-ta-ta

     ta

     ta . . .

~

now
I suppose that you know
a dragonfly
takes some
manoeuvring

on her own
she just wants to buck
and to sheer off
in tight angled
turns

I called mine
isosceles d-fly

she could
turn me around
on a dime

and she was nasty
whenever she met
an *emerald*
or a *tiger*
up in what she thought of
as her space

~

     . . . *ta*

     ta-ta-ta-ta . . .

~

it's a small world
you know
up
over the pond

a small jungle
but we called it
ours

and we believed
we had
no choice

that we had to fight
to keep our reeds
and water
and our air

in the end
though
I'm not so sure
I lost both
of my *'fly-boy*
brothers
in the length
of a single flight . . .

and *isosceles* fell
right out of the sky
gossamer wings
in tatters

and me with her

I'm still alive
but I'm bent now
into all the wrong angles

and
far as I can tell
the war
seems to be going on
just fine
even though
I'm not up there
~

    . . . *ta*
   ta-ta-ta-ta . . .

~

ahhhh
well

~

    . . . *ta*
    ta-ta-ta-ta . . .

~

ah well

~

    . . . *ta*
    ta-ta-ta-ta
    ta-ta-ta-ta
    ta-ta-ta
    ta
    ta

    ta
    ta-ta-ta-ta
    ta-ta-ta-ta
    ta-ta-ta
    ta

    ta . . .

~

ah
well

davey's interview (pre-recorded)

I used to play
all the time
when I was kid
you know . . .

around the edges
of our part of the pond

imagining
that one of the larvae —
a sleek looking nymph —
was mine

and that I
would get to train him
and he
would teach me

as we sort of
you know
grew up
together

and imagining
that I was up there
with the others

doing the sharp turns
and patrolling
around the boundaries

maybe fighting
some enemy 'fly

maybe
a whole squadron of them
all by myself

just me
and my jewel-wing

did I mention
I ended up paired
with a damsel

I call him ebony-blue
because of his wings
and his body

aw
I never did care much
what the fighting was about
you know

I only wanted . . .

always
I wanted to be up there

to own the sky

and wanted to win
whatever the heck
the fighting was about

now here I am
with my ebony blue best friend
and my 'fly-boy buddies

we're all
living the dream

anyway
I've got to go

the bad guys are coming after us
again
and some hero
and his damselfly
and his mates
needs to go
to sort them out

see ya

styx (across the road)

the fish has leapt
out of the stream

water
holds a touch
upon the tail

a possibility
in the event . . .

should there be a need
for returning

~

I
stand the prow

I pole ahead
avoiding both
rapids
and eddies

another man
in another boat
swims
with four wheels
more quickly turning

traffic
on this river
runs
both ways

~

the song
that the current sings
is the sound of the full wind
howling

the timbre of its melody
rises up in my own voice

at the same time
night

at the same time
mountain

~

I am boatman
on a river
wide

other men are
only so many
travellers

I choose a path
both deep and high

so come

and come
with . . .

there

right there
do you see

it is
the other side

the king and his courtier have a conversation

oh king

oh king

oh king of mine
what will you do
about dragons

what
will you do
about wyrms

call
for the brave

I will call
for the brave

let *them*
deal with this *wyrmin*

extinguish their fires
with lance
or with sword

the brave!

oh king

oh my good
king
the brave have all
left us

fallen into fire
or taken

oh king

dear king

what will you do
about dragons

treasure

I will give
my treasures
all

my golden cups

my gems

all of the worth
residing
in the treasury

give them
my treasure

oh king

oh my dear king

the treasury
is emptied

your coin is spent

on clothing
for courtiers
(for which
we thank you)

on feasting
and the necessity
of minstrels

pavilions
and fairs ...

what will you do
about
the wyrms

my daughters

my virtuous
daughters

let *them*
appease
these dragons

virtue so true
and chastity
pure

no dragon
could refuse
gifts
such as these

my daughters will

please them

oh king

oh
my king

I regret to inform
that . . .

no no
I cannot say
but . . .

what will you do
about
these dragons

guards

my faithful guards

take this man
and take
his mouth
into the mountain home
of these dragons

let him fill up
their ears
with woe

let him
inform them why
their fires
cannot achieve
their sundry goals

let him persuade

or
let him
fry

I care not
anymore

but
take this man
from my sight

his treacherous mouth
away
from my ears

a song for the (chosen) horizon

they talk about
a walk
in space

but
I don't know . . .

it's more like
a floating

a push
when I press
the button

forward
back
or up and down

>   choose a plane
>   that you will call
>   horizon
>
>   select a stance
>   that you know to be
>   standing
>
>   don't move
>   your legs
>
>   don't try
>   to swim
>   with the motion
>   of your arms
>
>   trust

place your faith
inside your suit
then pick out
a direction

and decide how fast
(go slow)

and decide how far
(the harness)

array your tools
the way you practiced
in the capsule

breathing
is such a wild thing
so loud
inside a helmet
that I can almost hear
the individual molecules
of my own inhaled air

men swear
there must be life
out here
but I
am not so sure

when you can sense
the way the vacuum
wants to kiss you
and when you can see
the squared result
of *nothing*
right before your eyes . . .

you know
then
what it means
to be alone

press a button

feel the thrust

creep along the job
until it is done

then turn around
push away
for home

stay on a level
with the relativity of your
personally chosen
horizon

unbound (goodbye)

gravity
would hold me down
but
I was not made
to be
earthly tied

I set my sights
somewhere
over the tree tops

the strength
my strength
lives
in the will I hold

my equivalent
of *musclebound*

and
gravity be damned
I slowly rise

I
am
as silence *is*

I am as *air*

I am
the blue above

I am as though
the cloud . . .

I

as though
over the trees
un bound

I wave
to gravity

goodbye

the message (of caprice)

down
onto my
knees

I drew a spark
from flintstone

leaning in
I blew
a soft breath

red glow . . .

to
twirl of smoke . . .

to
flame

gentle
I blew
to raise the fire

then green leaves
onto greener wood
to make the plumes
thicken blue

and green again
onto green . . .

so it was
I shaped
my source

and thick
it rose
so I rapidly
made the gestures
with my hands
that spoke the message

sent
up to the sky

~

caprice
is a day
that will not carry
any statements

caprice
is a breeze
that breaks my smoke
too small

too thin

caprice is the way
the words
my heart had sorely floated
are scattered . . .

confetti . . .

across the wide sky

and as I watched
the fire rose
hungry

devouring
the last phrase
of my appeal

94

in the end
sent *nowhere*

the rocket ship (in somnia)

there is a rocket
on the road outside

revving its thrusters
at me

calling me
to quit my shave
halfway
put on the helmet
to and clamp it
to the suit

I check myself
for reflections
back and forth
from visor
to mirror
to infinity in a bathroom

and there it goes
again

this time it's the feeling
of a hot breath exhaled
by an impatient machine
to rattle
at my window

my neighbours don't care

most everyone
is sleeping

and the rumbling
of my ship
is a lullaby

well all right
all right then
it is goodbye

goodbye

a journey to the stars
will not wait
for me to pack
yet another book
filled
with inspirations

> *here I come here I come*
> *there's still*
> *plenty of time*
>
> *hold your steam in*
> *you old grumbler*
>
> *all aboard*
> *let's go*
>
> *start up your shake*
> *and shudder*
>
> *ship . . .*
>
> *ship of mine*
> *aim me at a twinkle*
> *out of the black*
> *above*

I
will close my eyes
and try to sleep

you . . .

take me
away

abacus the stars

I've learnt to trust
the old abacus
to measure the miles
across space

I can't *really* use it
but manipulating the beads
on their wires
eases my mind

touching mountain ash
from the rainforest
near my home on earth
reassures me

we eat the light years
in this streak of motion
I am sitting in

I don't feel the movement —
don't get sick —
but I feel the tension
that comes of being propelled

how big
I wonder . . .

just how *big*
is the universe

why does it tolerate
me
and this ship

perhaps I should ask
a black hole
as we pass by it

there is only me
awake now

I am not at my best
when I'm alone

and I am
so
alone
with everybody ese
deep-sleeping

suspended

another month —
or whatever
seven hundred and twenty hours
should be called now —
until I am relieved
to get a little shut eye
of my own

forty three thousand
minutes
until *my* hibernation

and there is nothing
for me to do
except
some beaded non-calculations

on an abacus
that reminds me of a tree
from a home
I will never see
again

this universe is so big . . .

and *god*
it is *boring*

in the stone : through the water

a stone
thrown into deep
dark water . . .

not really
but I live
in the land of
perhaps

of
maybe

and
might have . . .

so it could be
that my little ship
is a stone
thrown into the deep water
of space

it is as dark
here
as any ocean

my ship and I
are as small
as a grain
of sea-washed sand

slowly spinning
in the long tide
of an eternity

.

.

.

    what about god

well
no man
has come closer

and

    what about the better world
    that is supposed to come

I *must* be
getting near it

and I wait

sometimes
quite calm

I wait

sometimes dismayed

I wait
just another soul
ready for the light

and I wait
for the *main* part
a patient man

that is the role
that is left
for me

awaiting
the light

otherwise
there is
nothing

od ovo

my name is
od ovo

from this place
you
seem very far away

everything
seems very far
away

mine . . .

ours
is the yellow one
the small stone
I get to call
my home

we're just
circling
around a star

to me it seems like
that
is *all* we do

and when a cycle takes
too long
I kick up the yellow dust
that lingers
in the dirty air
and clings to everything

unti. the scrubber
knocks it down

every *dark-time*
up there
in the night
I see a green moon –
a beauty —
turning

spinning

I don't know
if she
or we
are *really* the satellite

but
around she goes . . .

and around *I* go

I wish . . .

oh
how I wish
I was up there

anywhere
else
is the place
I want to be

anywhere but this
space-junk *asteroid*
of dust
and . . .

and
just *crap*

I reach out . . .

other stars are there
I reach out . . .

other planets

I reach
but
nothing reaches back

nothing wants
to touch *me*

I've heard stories
of places with h2o
just lying
on the ground

and
I've heard of this *water*
hanging
suspended
in the air

water
that makes *trees* grow

thick enough
to hide the ground
across half a planet

I think it could be
that the traveller-kind
tell little lies
to confound
a back-rock yokel
like they think I am

and anyway
I believe . . .

maybe
that I'm going to die
here
on this rock
and in this dust

right here

on *old yellow*

the total sum
of my every breath

~

my name
is *od ovo*

I have been
from here
for all of my life

my world
goes around
and around
a forlorn star

a song for the (deep) horizon

he keeps his eyes
closed tight
teeth clenched
against the pressure

strapped into his seat
he knows —
emotionally —
that he is burning

the darkness
in his capsule
is on fire

> *he wonders*
>
> *what is left of the soul*
> *to sacrifice*
> *in the sear*
> *of these flames*
>
> *what is left*
> *of the man*
> *who*
> *once upon a time*
> *left the earth*
>
> *who is*
> *the comet man*
> *re-entering on fire . . .*
>
> *a phoenix*
> *perhaps*

or some other bird
consumed in the night
by the sky

water
is like rock
when it is struck
by a blow
from above

water
is like cloud
like a mist
when it burns

silence
is *time* . . .

a wave
washing both the traveller
and his capsule ride

while the horizon —
at last —
is only a few feet
deep

and almost
within his grasp

Frank Prem

not sorry only grief (waiting)

*I have no wish
to go back
home*

*home
never
quite
had room
for what I was*

*it is enough
for me
to
remember*

*but
I do wish
that home
could spare a thought —
just occasionally —
for me*

the meeting
had gone on
and on

a long time

men and women
and dust

how long
was the burning question

how long
until relief . . .

and how long
until *home*
has had enough . . .

until the re-supply
should *fail* . . .

was the colony
meant
to be self-sufficient
so soon . . .

(it's too soon)

will home
care
what happens
in this far arm
anyway . . .

should they add
an *appeal*
to a prayer . . .

will *prayer*
take the place
of *grain* . . .

and if the store ship
doesn't come —
doesn't come
very soon —

what god is there
that will touch them
with a grace

~

this dust
lingers
so thickly
in the air

there are times
I need to go inside my shelter
just to inhale something
scrubbed clean

and I agree
totally
with what the man said . . .

with what we *all* said
and
while I am not sorry
yet
I grieve

the second beat

on a planet
where there stands
only *me*

the cosmos
has sounded a note

I don't know
if it was the only note
but
it is the only one
that I heard

it started
somewhere
way out there

way out
when

ended up somewhere —
some-when —
inside of me

and I felt it

and I heard it

and I knew
I was not
alone

the sound
is a thing that
is the first beat
of a song

and I know
that *I*
am the next beat

and that the song
cannot be played
by one note
alone

the words
cannot be sung . . .

without *me*

even here
on a planet where
I
am *the only one*
the first note
needs
to hear me
and feel me

in the same way
that I
can hear
and can feel
that first note

and know
where I
belong

Author Information

Frank Prem has been a storytelling poet since his teenage years. He has been a psychiatric nurse through all of his professional career, which now exceeds forty years.

He has been published in magazines, online zines, and anthologies in Australia, and in a number of other countries, and has both performed and recorded his work as spoken word.

Frank is an Adjunct Research Associate of the School of Education, Charles Sturt University, Australia.

He lives with his wife in the beautiful township of Beechworth in North East Victoria, Australia.

Connect with Frank

Find Frank at his website www.FrankPrem.com, or through Social Media online at Facebook, X (Twitter), Instagram and YouTube.

Other Published Works

Free Verse Poetry

Small Town Kid (2018)
Devil In The Wind (2019)
The New Asylum (2019)
Herja, Devastation - With Cage Dunn (2019)
Walk Away Silver Heart (2020)
A Kiss for the Worthy (2020)
Rescue and Redemption (2020)
Pebbles to Poems (2020)
The Garden Black (2022)
A Specialist at The Recycled Heart (2022)
Ida: Searching for The Jazz Baby (2023)
From Volyn to Kherson (2023)
Alive Is What You Feel (2023)
White Whale (2024)
Pilgrim Volume 1 - Illustrated by Leanne Murphy (2024)
A Poetry Archive Volume 1 (2024)
A Poetry Archive Volume 2 (2024)
A Poetry Archive Volume 3 (2024)
A Poetry Archive Volume 3 (2024)

Picture Poetry/Spoken Image

Voices (In The Trash) (2020)
The Beechworth Bakery Bears (2021)
Sheep On The Somme (2021)
Waiting For Frank-Bear (2021)
A Lake Sambell Walk (2021)
A Few Places Near Home (2023)
The Cielonaut (2024)

What Readers Say

Small Town Kid

A modern-day minstrel. Highly recommended.
 —A. F. (Australia)

Small Town Kid is a wonderful collection.
 —S. T. (Australia)

Devil In The Wind

Trust me, this book will stay with you. Bravo!
 —K. K. (USA)

Moving, beautiful, and terrible. I was left with a profound sense of respect, as well as a reminder that we should never take for granted every precious every moment of life.
 —J. S. (South Africa)

The New Asylum

Words can't do justice to the emotional journey I travelled in (reading this collection).
 —C. D. (Australia)

If I had to pick one book over the past year that has truly resonated with me, this would be it.
 —K. B. (USA)

Walk Away Silver Heart

Instantly grips you by the throat in his step-by-step story of survival. Bravo!
 —K. K. (USA)

Outstanding!
 —B. T. (Australia)

A Kiss For The Worthy

A Celebration of Life Written in Thoughtful Bursts of Poetic
Expression
 —C M C (United States)

With every verse, I found myself reflecting about myself, my life,
and the world.
 —K

Rescue and Redemption

The passion of love in its many forms explored by one for another.
 —J L (United States)

I've enjoyed every word, every breath. Every moment within the life
of these stories.
 —C D (Australia)

Sheep On The Somme

Museums and archivists take note~sell this in your gift shops,
preserve it in your archives. Professors, teachers~share with your
students.
 —A R C (United States)

(This) book is a beautiful and graphic tribute to all those brave men
and women who gave their lives for their countries between 1914
and 1918.
 —R C (South Africa)

Ida: Searching for The Jazz Baby

I found myself deeply moved by the presentation of Ida's elusive,
illusionary life.
 —E G (United States)

He gives her a depth and vulnerability that the press didn't.
 — A C (United Kingdom

The Garden Black

Prem creates verse that illuminates our world, its experiences and history.

  —S C (United Kingdom)

Prem's poetry reminds that life is fragile and fleeting ... both harsh and beautiful.

  —D G K (Canada)

A Few Places Near Home

The author has captured many beautiful images in this book, and is a wonderful photographer as well as a poet. This book would make a beautiful coffee table book filled with moving prose to make us ponder with gorgeous accompanying images.

  —D K (Canada)

www.FrankPrem.com